Eminence

—

Hope Beyond Series

—

Nadine C. Keels

Eminence

© 2012 by Nadine C. Keels

—

Cover Design: Nadine C. Keels

—

—

Find Nadine C. Keels online at:
www.prismaticprospects.wordpress.com

Nadine. A French name, meaning, "hope."

Nadine C. Keels is an author and blogger with a lifelong passion for the power of story. She writes the kinds of stories she wants to read but can't always find, and her aim is to spark hope and inspiration in as many people as she can reach.

—

<u>Malt Shop Milestones Series</u>
Vicky's Victory | Berta's Bounceback | Ari's Aria

—

<u>Crowns Legacy Series</u>
Reviving the Commander | Embracing the Outcast

—

<u>Eubeltic Realm Series</u>
Eubeltic Descent | Eubeltic Quest | Eubeltic Virtue | Eubeltic Outliers

—

<u>Hope Beyond Series</u>
Eminence | Simplicity

—

<u>Movement of Crowns Series</u>
The Movement of Crowns | The Movement of Rings | The Movement of Kings

—

<u>For Every Love Series</u>
Love Unfeigned | Hope Unashamed | Kiss and 'Telle?

—

<u>Heartstrings Series</u>
We Were Real | A Christmas So Real

—

<u>Jhoi Series</u>
World of the Innocent | World of Joy

—

Love by the Breather: Four Romantic Reads

Chapter One

"WE HAVE WON! WE HAVE won!"

Ahnna's ears prickled as soon as the faint sound of vibrant shouts outside reached her hearing. Her head flew up from its bent position over a steaming washtub full of clothing, wisps of wavy hair that had loosened from her chignon sticking to her damp neck. Her mother, Delmi, looked up the second that she did, the two women staring wide-eyed at each other before Ahnna dropped the soaking garment she had been scrubbing and bolted out of the laundering room, the resulting hot splash of water missing the skirt of her thin, dark purple day robe and splattering onto the wooden floor. Delmi left her tub as well, following her daughter through their large village farmhouse and out of the front door, Delmi stopping on the porch while Ahnna lifted her skirts to run down the stone walk, through the gate, and into the street.

Sure enough, others from nearby houses were being drawn to the street as the shouts became more pronounced. Ahnna looked toward the late afternoon sunlight pouring over the crest of a hill to the west as a band of hollering boys in blue uniforms

1

came streaming down the hill, some of them waving sticks madly through the air. "*We have won!*"

As the messenger boys approached, most of them being adolescent pupils of Ahnna's, she fleetingly thought that she hadn't seen them so animated since the announcement earlier in the year that community classes had been postponed in anticipation of a colonial crisis. Ahnna dashed down the road to take one of the boys by the shoulders, not even thinking to dodge his wagging stick, unknowingly escaping a potential blow. She had no chance to ask the boy anything before he exulted in her face, "Magistra! The battle at Mtihani is over! The enemy will have to surrender. We have won our independence!"

The boy jumped up to stamp an impulsive kiss on his schoolmistress's cheek before he carried on and away with his young, triumphant compatriots. The street was teeming with neighbors by this time, the usual tasks of the day put on pause as an astounded clamor arose that did not immediately strike Ahnna's hearing as celebratory. In truth, the clamor and commotion barely struck her at all as she stood in the middle of the road, unseeingly looking after the departing band of boys. "Our independence," she whispered to no one.

Over the past three years, she'd been eating the revolution. She'd been drinking the revolution. She'd been sleeping and dreaming the revolution. And she knew she was by no means the only one in the country who'd been doing so. Could this merciless, bloody ordeal finally be finished?

Ahnna walked slowly back toward her house, stopping at the gate in a daze. It wasn't until she looked over to again meet the now shining eyes of her mother, who hadn't left the porch, that she realized the noise of their surrounding neighbors was that of rejoicing.

Independence.

Ahnna's eyes could not help but to contract the infectious shine of Delmi's, but both women knew there wasn't much time to engage in festivity. The close proximity of their village to the various zones of combat, once toward the north but now toward the west, not only meant that they were commonly the first to receive news on the war, but it also meant that the village would shortly be met with the urgent pounding of horses' hooves and the rumbling of wagons' wheels as another influx of wounded warriors would be brought into the area. The swarm of men would need direct attention in houses here before they could be sent on to their own villages. Daichi, Ahnna's father, would soon be returning for the day as well, as he would have left his watch near the battlefield when the fighting ended. Everyone here would have to prepare.

Albeit the preparations, while there was still much to be looked after following combat, would bear something different now: an added sense of burgeoning relief that they had at least seen through this to an end. Sometimes an ending, whether that of loss or victory or a mixture of both, was an unassuming reward all by itself.

The house of Daichi relapsed into the state of "half-home, half-infirmary" that it had often been in during those three years, while the fighting had leapt back and forth against the edges of the region. Ahnna was not unfamiliar with tending to farmhands, when they would come in from Daichi's fields with minor injuries from working, but prior to the revolution, she had never been exposed to the kind of harm that warfare could inflict upon a human body. She loathed to imagine what the soldiers themselves must have been obligated to see out there. She declined from asking her father to give specific details about what he would witness while he was out on lowland battlefield watch, as he was one of the prophets appointed to be on hand in support of the commandants on duty. Ahnna did notice, however, that her father's long, peppery hair grew increasingly gray in hardly any time, and sluggishness hampered his gait more frequently.

The infirmary arrangement at the farmhouse had been unnerving to Ahnna at the beginning of the war, but after closely watching and following the lead of her mother, something she had learned to do from the time she had been adopted into this family, Ahnna had steadily grown accustomed to her nursing role.

This time, apparently to be the last time, six soldiers were brought to the house to be cared for. Delmi sent Ahnna out to the village square one morning to purchase more ingredients for salve, for the soldiers' wounds. While Ahnna was in the square, it was not the first occasion in her life when she had to stop what she was doing, turn toward a young man and woman standing together in the square, and lower her head. The other patrons in the square, when they saw what was taking place, did likewise. The young man had untied and removed his principal, the thin robe often worn over a man's leisure or formal clothing, and he was placing the robe over the maiden's shoulders. It was the traditional way of paying official suit, with the bowed heads around signifying the community's respect for it.

Ahnna could understand the man's timing, as he had likely fought in the war and wanted to make haste in asking his beloved to marry him.

The present witnesses were free to lift their heads when the man and woman began to walk off together, a good number of the people becoming well-wishers for the departing couple. Ahnna would have liked to join in with the sudden and brief bout of merriment, but she had to hurry back home with the salve ingredients she'd procured.

Over the next several days, the village doctor made regular visits to the Daichi house. Three of the soldiers there became well enough to be taken home. Two of them died. One of them, who'd been brought in unconscious from a head wound he'd sustained, did not regain stable consciousness until a week after the other soldiers were gone. Even then, every moment awake, he spent in silence, appearing perplexed. Every moment in sleep, he appeared to be in pain.

During one evening while the soldier lay sleeping on his mat on the floor of a side room, and Ahnna vigilantly sat close by, cutting out cloth to be used for fresh bandages, she overheard her father and the doctor in the wide foreroom in the middle of the house. They were discussing the house's one remaining war patient.

"It makes no sense for him to have gone out to fight," the doctor asserted. "He did his part for our military in his youth. He has helped to train enough younger men under him."

Daichi chuckled. "You speak of him as if he is an elderly fool. He is quite younger than you are, old friend. And younger than me and my—what have you called them?—my 'lagging' bones. I have told my proximate successor in the village to be ready, but not too ready, to take my place, seeing how you seem set to write me and my bones off."

"Oh, your blessed bones are only part of the problem, as far as your health goes. You simply do not have the body you had in your prime, decades ago, despite how much you try to ignore it. But let us leave you out of this, shall we? I do not speak of Ikenna as elderly. I speak of him as a man who has already paid his dues on the field. He helped to make us ready for revolution, and everyone knows and thinks much of him for it. But he should not have gone to the front lines. We need him at his estate now, being a master of trade, using that brain of his. The profeta in his village should have told him that, Daichi. You would have."

"Now, do not blame any of the profeti. We agreed on what we heard: 'Every man who is able and willing.' Ikenna is still able, and he was more than willing. He chose to fight."

"Yes. He chose to fight," the doctor grunted, "and now he is in there lying on your floor, paying for the fight with his damaged dome."

Daichi laughed again. "You know, medicus, for one in your healing profession, you can be most cynical."

"That I know. You have told me so enough times. Remind me to stuff my ears with socks before you say it again tomorrow." The doctor waited for his friend to finish laughing before he continued. "But you know what I mean. In some ways, Ikenna is a man still living in the past. He should be done with the field, should be raising a family."

"It is not his fault his wife died childless. She might have been like Delmi."

"You cannot be serious. No, it is not his fault, but yes, that was nigh on twenty years ago. He was fresh out of boyhood when he married, was younger than your daughter is now, and he was not married for long. I am telling you, he needs to concentrate on his business—and lecturing, if he is to go on with that—and raise up an heir for his estate. Leave the battlefields to the youth, I always say."

Daichi replied with a sigh. "Hopefully, we can all leave the battlefields for some time, good man. We have warred. So we must rest, and in peace revisit the reasons why we have fought. Ecclesiastical freedom. Autonomy in trade. An unrepressed exchange of ideas. No one else can decide for us what this nation will be. We now have the control to do that for ourselves, and so we must stay focused."

"Yes, we must. I agree."

Ahnna nodded unspoken concurrence, especially on the point regarding rest, feeling that her father was as much in need of rest from all of this as anyone. She knew the doctor had advised Daichi to give his complaining bones and joints an extended respite.

As the conversation in the other room turned to separate matters, Ahnna's eyes moved to the sleeping soldier on the floor. She'd heard mention of this Ikenna a number of times before, knowing him to be a regional administrator over the country's trade, as well as a public lecturer on the need for the industry's expansion. But she had never seen him in person herself until he'd been brought to the Daichi house, inert and covered in blood and muck. Delmi had had the task of getting rid of his ruined battle attire, and she'd found a small piece of parchment tucked safely under an inner fold of his shirt. Judging it to be a personal missive of some sort, Delmi had given it to Ahnna, telling her daughter to keep it for the soldier until he regained consciousness.

Watching the presently fitful breathing of this man, Ahnna knew that his soul hadn't been scrubbed clean of the soil of warfare when his injured body had. As he had yet to speak or to show any sign of recognition for words that were spoken to him, no one was sure if his memory and cognitive thinking were intact. Ahnna wondered, with some pity, if he would wind up going the way of the two soldiers who recently hadn't made it back out of the Daichi house. She was aware that it took will for a man to survive something like this, and there was no indication that Ikenna had much of it.

Later that night in her own side room, Ahnna did not know how long she'd been dozing before she was awakened by groaning noises. She left her pallet, grabbing a shawl to wrap over her light gown. Taking up a bowl of water that she'd been keeping near her, she hurried to go look in on Ikenna, making out in the darkness that he had rolled off of his mat onto his stomach. He lay there stiff and unmoving, but then he jerked violently, mumbling unintelligible words.

"Oh, God, he is stuck in a nightmare." Ahnna lit a lamp sitting on a table by the window and crossed over to kneel beside Ikenna, looking down into his face, flinching at his next, sudden jerk. He groaned another time, and Ahnna put the bowl down, bringing her hair over one shoulder to get it out of the way before putting a gentle hand on Ikenna's bare back.

"Sir?" she murmured but was caught off guard when Ikenna's dark eyes instantly flew open. She quickly leaned down so that he could see her clearly. "It is me, again, Ahnna," she identified herself to him as she had every time he'd been awake in her presence. "Do not be alarmed, please."

Ikenna stared at her, breathing heavily, his reddened eyes seemingly unable to focus.

"Would you like to lie back on the mat?" Ahnna asked him. "I will help you." She made her way around to his other side so that she could help him turn over without pushing him. Once he was on the mat, Ahnna pulled his blanket back up to his middle and placed the back of her hand on his damp face, which hadn't been shaved for some time. She gingerly touched the bandages wrapped around his head, concerned by their excessive warmth. "Hmm. Either you have only worked up a sweat in your sleep, or your fever may be trying to come back." She reached for the bowl of water, dipping her fingers into it, feeling the soaking cloth inside. The water wasn't as cold as it had been earlier, but she reasoned that it was considerably cooler than Ikenna's skin. She carefully folded his bandages back a bit, wrung out the cloth, and began dabbing it over his face and neck. "I added some lavender to your water, you see. I thought it might be soothing."

She met Ikenna's bemused gaze. "You look as if you do not believe I am here," she said, his obvious ambivalence making her inwardly question precisely what Mtihani must have been like for him, if he indeed remembered it. After putting the cloth back in the bowl, Ahnna took one of Ikenna's hands into both of her own. "Well, I certainly am here. Here with you in the house of Daichi, my father, on his farm. You are safe."

Ikenna gave no response, and so Ahnna went on to ask him, "May I show you something?" She let go of Ikenna's hand and reached beneath the edge of his mat, pulling out a small, folded piece of parchment. "Do you recognize this?"

She held the parchment up where he could see it, and his eyes widened slightly. Ahnna drew a reassured breath at this signal of memory from him. "You know the other woman who cares for you here, Delmi, my mother? She told me to keep this for you, but I must offer you an apology, sir. It was not any affair of mine, but I allowed my curiosity to get the better of me, and I opened this, days ago, to see what it was. Please forgive me for taking the liberty." Unfolding the parchment then, she commenced to read aloud from it, reciting the passages of Scripture that were written on it, poetic expressions of enduring hope during impermanent adversity.

Not all of the distress had departed from Ikenna's stare, but Ahnna did notice when his breathing calmed. When Ahnna had finished the passages, she read them through once more for emphasis, glancing up a few times to be sure that Ikenna was still listening. Then she refolded the parchment, slipping it beneath the edge of his mat, near his head. "I take it that those are treasured verses of yours. I put them here so you will know right where they are. Now, may I ask you to do something for me? May I ask you to get some more sleep?" She retrieved the cool cloth, continuing to dab at Ikenna's face and neck with it, sensing his reluctance. "Oh, I know it has not been the most enjoyable thing for you. I...I know you have been having bad dreams, sir. I can only imagine what these past years must have been for you, but, you see, you are here now. You are getting better, and I am sure that everyone back in your village misses you. They are glad you are alive. Think of the homecoming you will have. And for now, come morning, I or my mother will be right in to check on you. Perhaps you will feel like eating then, a little more than you have of late, to get your strength back up. Will you try?"

Ahnna gently dabbed at Ikenna's chest and bruised arms as well and then dropped the cloth back in the bowl, seeing that while Ikenna's eyelids were wavering, he was yet refusing sleep. At that point, Ahnna could have shaken her head at his resistance. She moved to kneel at the crown of his head, softly taking both sides of his bearded face into her hands, her hair now spilling forward over both of her shoulders. She smiled at Ikenna from her upside-down post, yielding to a comic impulse as she started to sing, unskillfully.

> *Hawks and geese only get so far by walking*
> *and how far might a horse or tiger crawl?*
> *A fool of a farmer would waste his days talking*
> *and never rise from his idle rump at all.*

It was a folksong that usually got a self-conscious titter out of pupils she chided in song for not completing their assignments on time, and she could tell that at her humor, Ikenna relaxed further. Ahnna laughed. "There, now. I am no songbird. But I will have no choice but to persist if you do not go on to sleep, sir."

Ikenna squinted up into the countenance of this young woman hovering over him, and then he closed his eyes.

Ahnna held back more laughter as she released the man's face and stood up, pulling her shawl more tightly around her. Instead of picking up the bowl of water or going to blow out the lamp, she stepped over between Ikenna's mat and the wall, sitting down, drawing her knees up, making sure her gown covered her legs. She leaned back against the wall, hoping that Ikenna would understand as she slid her feet close to where his hand lay on the mat, scooting her toes underneath his palm. His face turned toward her, and though he did not open his eyes, he allowed his hand to enclose loosely around one of her feet.

Daichi forgive her if this was not the most proper way to take care of a wounded man. She did not have the heart to leave him there, alone with his nightmares, and she did not fall asleep until she was sure that he had.

Unbeknownst to Ahnna, Delmi entered the room after dawn and halted, seeing her daughter sitting asleep against the wall, the soldier's large hand all but swallowing up her little foot. With the trace of a smile, Delmi backed out of the room.

Chapter Two

IN THE DAYS THAT FOLLOWED, although Ahnna was not informed of it, it was by collective agreement between Daichi, Delmi, and even the doctor that Ahnna was given the better part of the task of nursing Ikenna, gradually more in her mother's place. While Ikenna did not speak, he no longer appeared to be confused while he was awake, and Ahnna could generally read him when he looked at her. There were a couple more occasions when she was awakened to hear Ikenna groaning in his sleep, and she would go to speak to him until he was again quietly resting. She found she wasn't certain how much Ikenna was actually listening to her each time, but he did not seem to mind her going on as she did.

In reality, Ikenna was always listening to Ahnna. There was something youthful and ingenuous about her and her voice, and yet she was not without grace and self-possession. Living through the effects of the revolution had to have done its part in seasoning her. At moments, her words gave Ikenna space to drift: to drift back to when his lovingly strict parents were still alive; to drift to his military training that had begun while he was only a boy, right alongside his schooling; to drift to the many pranks he'd pulled with his comrades as a young man, before he'd met his wife, a woman now deceased; to drift to the estate he'd inherited from his parents and the party of faithful people living there who were undoubtedly keeping it running in his absence. He did miss his home. Yet, he was at peace about not being able to be there, for a while longer. Ahnna's manner toward him helped, in that respect.

Then, one afternoon while a talkative Ahnna was feeding Ikenna, who was sitting up against the wall, Ahnna let out an astonished, pleased laugh when Ikenna unexpectedly smiled in reaction to her chatter. Ahnna put down the bowl of steamed vegetables and noodles she'd been holding and took Ikenna's face into her hands with delight. "Sir, this is the most alive I have seen you look since you were brought here."

Ikenna only sat there for a moment before his hands came up to lower hers from his face, but when he did not let go of them, Ahnna felt her cheeks grow slightly warm. She'd been touching him so much lately, salving his wounds and whatnot, that she hadn't been compelled to think much of her doing so, until now. Ikenna's eyes shone with silent laughter as he spoke to her for the first time, his voice guttural from lack of use, his words slow. "Seeing me so alive causes you to blush?"

Ahnna choked on an amazed, embarrassed chortle. Her head shook. "Oh, no, it is not—I am just surprised."

"Surprised? At what?"

"Well, surprised that you would, um..." Ahnna wiggled her captive hands.

Ikenna's hold slackened somewhat. "Is this familiar of me?" he asked. "You have behaved familiarly with me for days, I do not know how many. You speak to me as a friend would."

"Oh. Yes. But, I had started to think that perhaps I have been talking too much."

"No, not at all. I am getting used to your voice. You have been so kind to me, I should be thanking you for your efforts each day, instead of holding my tongue."

Ahnna absorbed the apparent fact that he had been refraining from speaking quite intentionally. "It is perfectly fine," she told him. "I am able to distinguish your appreciation. And, if I may say so, I have appreciated you as well. No one, except my longest friend Hsiu Mei, listens to me go on so." Ahnna felt more instantaneous embarrassment over issuing that disclosure, unplanned, and seeing the laughter again in Ikenna's gaze, she slipped her hands out of his. "So. Our medicus gave us orders to allow your bruised arms to be still and heal." She took up the bowl of food, holding it out to him. "But, um, it appears that you can try feeding yourself for me, yes?"

Ikenna's smile was small, but warm. He accepted the bowl from her.

As Ikenna went on eating, Ahnna deemed it unnecessary for her to remain so close to him. She made ready to move away, but Ikenna extended one hand, touching her arm. "Stay, please, if you will. I do welcome your company."

"Do you?" Ahnna asked as his hand left her arm.

"Yes. You remind me of the blossoms that grow on the trees in my gardens, at home. Such soft vibrancy. I know it is the season for them to bloom, and not for the first time since the revolution broke out, I am missing it happen."

"Oh, dear. Then you must be anxious to get back home."

"Not overly anxious. Your presence here has been refreshing." Ikenna's eyes somberly lowered to the bowl in his hands. "You seem always to know when I am thinking of Mtihani."

Feeling her heart constrict at his words, Ahnna advised Ikenna, in a hushed voice, "You should eat more, sir. You must rebuild your strength."

Ikenna looked up at her. "I have gained much strength by your being here, Ahnna. I hope I might be able to return your kindness."

"Ahnna? You know my name?"

"Of course I do. You have introduced yourself to me several times since I have been here, have you not? I am sorry for not conveying to you that I understood. And I do know that you know my name as well, although you insist upon only calling me 'sir.'"

Ahnna could feel her flush deepening. "I would not presume to call you anything else. I do not know you that well."

"Hm. That can be corrected."

Ahnna could think of nothing to say to that assertion, so she simply watched Ikenna as he resumed his meal.

Ikenna, his senses sharp from years of conditioning, was alert to the fact that Daichi had been standing halfway through the door of the room for some minutes, but as Ahnna did not seem to know of her father's attendance, Ikenna made no mention of it, not even after Daichi left. Later that evening, while Ahnna was off helping Delmi to prepare supper, Daichi brought shears and a razor into Ikenna's room.

Ahnna was taken aback when she walked in with Ikenna's supper afterwards, seeing that he'd been shaved down to a light beard and had been given a haircut, his head now free from bandages. "Your father said it was time to find my face again, behind the thick of the forest."

Ahnna nodded. "I see." She walked over with Ikenna's tray of food. "I will have to commend him for that."

Ikenna ran a hand over his chin. "I suppose I must have looked terrible."

"Not terrible," Ahnna remarked, kneeling down and passing Ikenna the tray, "just old, I think."

It did not sound as if her comment was meant with any insolence or reproach, but it gave Ikenna pause. Did Ahnna consider him to be an old man? He would not have thought so previously, given that he plainly was not as old as her father, but now Ikenna could not say he was sure about it.

Ahnna would one day marvel at the amount of time she and Ikenna started spending in conversation, after the day of their first exchanges. Ikenna asked her questions about her studies, her teaching, and her pupils, as well as her gardening work and her pursuit of painting. Ahnna listened as Ikenna spoke of his business as a tradesman and his grounds at home, his village, and his relatives, which led to Ahnna's telling him about her adoption.

"Daichi and Delmi are not your natural parents?" Ikenna asked, surprised.

"No. Delmi has never given birth to a child. If you can believe it, in strictly natural terms, I am a native of the empire we just won our independence from." Ahnna's smile was ironic. "Hsiu Mei tells me there are flashes of moments when one can see I am not from around here. She says that I do not walk like the other women here do, that I do not tie my sashes correctly." Ahnna ran an absent hand over the sash of the coral day robe she was wearing. "But my mother does not have any problem with how I wear my clothing. She and my father say that I am special, but they never say that I am different.

"What is more, it is not as if I recall much from where I came from. I was very young, traveling with a caravan moving through this country. The man and woman who were my parents did not want me from the time I was born, saying so when they left me with a letter at the orphanage in this village before they and the caravan moved on. Daichi found me, his 'little love,' there. He said that it only took a couple of times watching me 'graciously instructing the other children in play, without apology,' for him to know I was destined to be a magistra.

"And a magistra I have become. I am eager to restart my teaching this autumn. My boys and girls will have some catching up to do, what with the war interrupting classes once planting season was underway. And, although I am not a specialist in the dramatic arts, I am also looking forward to using the amateur theatre the village built beside the school, before the war. My children and I have yet to put anything on for our community."

"Ah, how fortunate. I have always been partial to the theatre. Well, you do love teaching, Ahnna—and your children. That I can see." Ikenna nodded slowly. "Nothing taken from my knack for business and civic duty, my parents knew I was born to be a warrior. Even in my current profession, I have not gotten away from it. Although, Mtihani had a way of letting me know it was my final battle. I have served my time."

Ahnna thought carefully before asking him, "Do you think you are going to miss it?"

Ikenna's look was dubious. "Miss Mtihani?"

"Oh, no, no—do you think you will miss being in the military?"

Ikenna peered down at his hands. Ahnna suspected that he was not going to answer her, but he eventually met her eyes with a fervency reminiscent of fire. "I will mourn no longer being in the field. I believe in this land. The moral principles that our people hold fast to are more than worth fighting for. I love the discipline that the military requires one to embrace swiftly. Being a sovereign nation, we will need more discipline than ever before. But I will not miss the horrors of war." His voice lowered to a grave mumble. "Mtihani was the one place that I seriously sensed would have killed me."

"Would have," Ahnna was quick to interject. "It only 'would have.' And 'would have' was not good enough. You played a vital role in bringing our victory out there. I am sorry you were not conscious the day our enemy signed the surrender agreement, but it was a glorious day. All things considered, it was a glorious day indeed. I heard tell that the Chief of State himself would have had you there at the signing, if you had been able to go. You should be proud, sir."

"Mm. Perhaps." Ikenna gave another slow nod. "Perhaps, one day, I will be proud. Today, I am just thankful that it is over."

Ahnna nearly reached out a compassionate hand to him, but she abstained from doing so. Ikenna perceived her aborted gesture, but he did not speak of it. He had noted, to his unreasonable yet marked disappointment, that the more his health improved, the less Ahnna would touch him.

By the time he could walk around relatively well on his own and was fit enough to be treated as a real guest in the Daichi house, he did not object to the fact that neither the master of the house nor his wife made mention of Ikenna's returning to his village right away.

On an afternoon when Ikenna declared his healing limbs' need for exertion, Ahnna suggested that he accompany her on a walk to Hsiu Mei's house, as Ahnna hadn't seen much of Hsiu Mei or her family since the end of the war. "She lives right past the lake near the school—if you believe you can handle the walk, Ikenna."

Ikenna agreed to go out and be introduced to Ahnna's friend, and on their walk through the streets, Ikenna gained direct evidence of how much the village schoolmistress was admired by the people here. She shared several jovial smiles and greetings with adults and children alike, and Ikenna could not ignore the attracted glances Ahnna received from more than one young man working in the village square. As they were passing the lake, Ahnna asked Ikenna how he was holding up, and he assured her that he was fine.

Hsiu Mei seemed pleased to make Ikenna's acquaintance upon his arrival at her house, but when he turned to meet her other family members who were present, Hsiu Mei gave Ahnna a look both telling and inquisitive behind the man's back. Ahnna determinedly shook her head, using the first second she knew she wouldn't be overheard to whisper to her friend, "He has been recovering from battle at my father's house. That is *all*."

"Oh? He looks plenty recovered to me," Hsiu Mei whispered back. "Did he offer to escort you out and about today?"

"Nonsense. Cannot you see he still walks with a limp and moves his arms woodenly? He was merely in need of exertion today."

"But he is wearing a leisure principal of your father's, yes?"

"No. My mother made that one for Ikenna, to help him feel more at home until he leaves. Now, enough of this."

Hsiu Mei smiled and said no more, for the time being.

As days at the farmhouse passed, Daichi and Delmi kept close watch over Ikenna and their daughter. Daichi observed how Ikenna would accept proffered books from the study to read with Ahnna in the evenings, and Delmi observed, during vegetable gardening times, that Ahnna took many glances over into the field where Ikenna had begun working with Daichi's farmhands, as he gradually became able.

Moreover, Daichi and Delmi both noticed when Ahnna took up calling Ikenna by his given name.

Ikenna summoned a messenger boy one day to send word to a village courier, providing instructions for something he wished to retrieve from his estate. Around dusk on the next day, he was glad to see the messenger boy arrive with the items he had asked for. While the Daichi family was sitting out on the front porch after supper, Ikenna, with a deep bow, presented Daichi and Delmi with a detailed piece of blown glass with gemstones set in it, depicting a branch of blossoms. "Profeta, and domina, I wish to thank you both for your benevolence and hospitality. Had we been at my home, I would have liked to personally usher you on a walk to see the actual blossoms on the trees in my gardens," Ikenna admitted, "but I am sure the petals are mostly fallen, by now. This is from the mantelpiece in my library. I would like you both to have it."

Then, Ikenna presented Ahnna with a glass branch as well, telling her, "This is for the hours you have spent restoring me back to health. The gift is not equivalent to the level of your great kindness, but I do hope you might find in it at least a measure of the pleasure I have found in your company."

Daichi and Delmi watched as their daughter smiled, thankfully accepting the branch, and, blushing, rose to her feet. "I must go find a suitable place for this," she announced as she left the porch to enter the house. Ikenna excused himself from the porch also, and the husband and wife left outside shared a look. Delmi's brows lifted, and Daichi nodded in response.

In the house, Ikenna found Ahnna in the entryway outside of the foreroom. She, examining one of the walls, told Ikenna she would mount her branch there, with her parents' branch on the opposite side, if they agreed to it. Ahnna turned to face Ikenna, her movement causing a tendril of wavy hair to flutter against her temple. Ahnna reached up to smoothly tuck the tendril behind her ear, and Ikenna thought to himself that at that instant, she looked as youthful and ingenuous as ever, yet with a womanly poise he could not help but to view with his ever-heightening degree of fascination.

"Thank you again for the gift, Ikenna," Ahnna said. "You must be all the more anxious to get back home to your gardens, and to your party of people on the estate and all of your neighbors, at that. But, if I may confess so much, I do believe something will be missing here, when you are gone."

Ikenna felt an unanticipated pang of regret. "Oh, I am sure you will not miss me. You will be busy handling all of the fellows in the area who have been waiting to pay suit to you, while you have been shut away in the house with us lingering war casualties."

When he saw Ahnna's eyes broaden while the rest of her went still, Ikenna ruefully wondered where his remark had come from. He'd never stopped to think in earnest about Ahnna probably having suitors, so his own words took him off guard. He now considered how Ahnna had never mentioned anything to him about suitors, he hadn't heard anyone in the household say anything on the subject, and no suitors that he knew of had made any appearances at the Daichi house since his coming.

However, seeing the way Ahnna averted her eyes from him in clear unease, Ikenna asked himself if it were possible that any men had come to see her in the past but had had their plans delayed by the war. What if, somewhere within those three years, she had formed an attachment with some other wounded man who had been brought to the Daichi house for treatment? There was no guarantee that Ahnna had not had any male visitors while Ikenna had been lying in the house, unconscious. The aftermath of combat might not have provided the most romantic opportunity for a man to come calling on a woman, but Ahnna had told Ikenna about the betrothal she had seen established in the village square only days after Mtihani. A time dubbed as "postwar" seemed to be a desirable time to secure marriage prospects.

And Ahnna looked so uncomfortable now. Ikenna was well aware of his own station. It was not an impossibility that he, being widely esteemed, unmarried, and staying at the Daichi residence, could be hindering the advance of potential suitors who were looking out for his departure. If Ahnna did happen to have any particular fellow waiting to pay suit to her, and she would be glad to have Ikenna out of the way for that purpose, it would give one explanation why she had restated that Ikenna must be anxious to get back home, despite his saying before that he wasn't so much.

Ikenna inwardly rebuked himself for the direction of his thoughts. Any suitors of Ahnna's, actual or imagined, should not necessarily be any concern of his.

Meanwhile, Ahnna was looking everywhere in the entryway but at Ikenna, wondering what would have caused him to make his last comment. She thought their friendship had been developing nicely, and though she tried not to dwell on it, she could tell that Ikenna admired her as a woman. She admired him also, more than she was ready to acknowledge. She knew that, beneath his equanimity, there resided in him a well of passion, of zeal for his convictions. He was attentive and could bring the color to her face, with a word or less, as no one else could. Surely he wouldn't be so relaxed with the idea of other men calling on her, would he? Or could it be that Ikenna had never had a serious thought of paying suit to her himself?

Ahnna inwardly rebuked herself for the direction of her thoughts. She reminded herself that even if Ikenna had been thinking of paying suit to her, she did not know how she would, with a settled conscience, be able to accept it from him.

For the two of them to break out of this awkward moment, it took Ikenna's request for a trip to the study. Ahnna gave him a relieved smile at the chance for this diversion, but as they went and spent time reading together, Ahnna's relief waned as she perceived the added reservation in Ikenna's manner. She was not happy to find that she was grateful to get away from him, when she retired for the night.

The next day, while Ahnna and Delmi were out working in the vegetable garden, Ahnna didn't give much thought to her mother's sudden claim that she needed to get the two of them some cups of water until Ahnna looked up and saw Ikenna approaching from the back porch as Delmi disappeared inside of the house. Ahnna glanced toward the fields, asking Ikenna, "You are not going to work with the farmhands today?"

"Oh, no." Ikenna shook his head, stopping before Ahnna. "I am preparing to return to my estate."

"Are you? Already?"

"Already? Ahnna, I have been here for months. My gifts of branches to you all were parting gifts. I sent word out early this morning, telling my party to expect me tonight or tomorrow."

A silence ensued. Ahnna was searching for words to make up for her rudeness in not immediately wishing Ikenna well on his journey home when he came out with, "Ahnna, I must humbly beg your pardon for the blundering comment I made to you, yesterday evening. Your sacrifice of time, skill, and heart on behalf of the men who have been wounded in battle is praiseworthy. As far as suitors may go, if I was going to mention them, I should have said that in my becoming better acquainted with you, I can most certainly see why a fellow in the area, or any area, would want to pay suit to you."

Ahnna rapidly blinked a few times, thanking Ikenna and disallowing herself the opportunity to become subsequently speechless by smiling a bit and candidly divulging, "But I cannot say that anything has ever been paid to me that one would call a suit. The seasons come and go, my well-liked parents receive honored guests, and suitors do make their rounds about the village, but never here. Not yet. I must own that the conditions in my home and my role in it over the past few years has not made this the most ideal place for suitors, though I have fulfilled my role without apology, as my father would say.

"But besides that, I think some of the fellows I grew up with might fear a booming otherworldly voice overhead and fiery lightning bolts from the heavens if ever they were to call on Daichi the sacred profeta's sacred daughter." Her smile widened with humor. "Either that, or my boys and girls have spread the news about their magistra's singing, and the dread of it is keeping all of the unattached men in the vicinity away from here."

Ikenna laughed aloud, remembering the night when Ahnna had crooned about hawks and lazy farmers to him. He knew that if he'd been in a different frame of mind that night, he would have laughed heartily back then. Indubitably, her singing had been dreadful to his ears. Ikenna took a moment to study her now, knowing that he had vaguely allowed the issue of their age disparity to weigh upon him too heavily. "Your father says that he would like for me to write to him."

Ahnna nodded. "That is wonderful. All the better to keep him consistently informed on trade developments. He will like that."

"Yes, I believe he will. And, for this I hope you will not think me presumptuous, but I went ahead and asked his blessing to write to you as well."

"Oh? To keep me also informed on trade?"

It took a second for Ikenna to realize Ahnna was teasing him. He grinned at her and took a step back, bowing to her. "If that is what you would prefer to call it."

Ahnna laughed, but not without some niggling discomfort, as Ikenna reached for something inside of his principal, stepping forward to press a piece of folded parchment into her hand. "I never said so, but I did forgive you for taking the liberty you once took with this," Ikenna stated, and with that, he excused himself from her, walking away toward the house. Ahnna recognized the parchment, but now something was written on the outside of it.

Hold fast to God. And remember me.

~Ikenna

This man was leaving little doubt as to what his intentions toward her were. Although the thought of his continued attentions elated her, Ahnna wondered if there might be a way to ward off any potential or rising amorousness without damaging their friendship. She in no way wanted to lose her connection with him.

It wasn't until Ikenna was inside of the house that Delmi came back outside, without any cups of water.

Later on, a chaise arrived to take Ikenna to his village. As he said his goodbyes to the Daichi family, Delmi watched the cordial, rather mild, farewell that passed between Ikenna and her daughter. The chaise took off, and once Ahnna turned and started back down the stone walk to the farmhouse, looking neither brilliantly joyful nor brilliantly wistful, Delmi discreetly held questioning hands up to her husband. Daichi sighed and nodded, putting an arm around his wife as they followed their daughter down the walk.

Chapter Three

"HE MUST HAVE ACQUIRED some new land, yes?"

"Yes. He must have. New land. The Chief of State may have rewarded him with some, for all of his service. He has received a mysterious letter from the State Escritoire. Might the letter speak of land?"

"New land would explain it," another from the party around the long banquet room table put forward. "Would not it explain it all, Hinuhinu? New land, or perhaps a new line of trade."

"Or perhaps a new mule," the addressed Hinuhinu piped in, a current of laughter from the party following his suggestion.

"Maybe he is just that glad about the end of the war, as we all are," one of the women at the table spoke up. "Maybe he is just happy to be alive."

"But our dominus has been in the military for a long time. He has come back from conflict before, happy to be alive. With all due respect to him, that would not explain the present change in him."

"His coming back is different this time, though. Never before had anything kept him away from home long after his duty like the effects of Mtihani did. It must be such a relief to him to have survived it and to be among us again."

"What do you think, Niyol? What would you say has happened to him?"

The addressed man named Niyol, who hadn't as yet added anything into the discussion, swallowed a bite of his dinner. "Well." He rearranged his bowls of food before him. "I am sure he will feel free to correct me if I am mistaken. But I would deem it safe to say that our dominus has gone..." He looked down into his bowl of soup, dipping his spoon into it. "...and fallen in love."

Every member of the estate party, except Niyol, turned toward the head of the table to stare at Ikenna, who had been wordlessly eating his meal as if he did not hear any of the conversation about him taking place, here in the banquet room of his home. The attention of the party members' children, who were dining at a separate table in the room, was soon drawn to the adults' table, on account of the jarring lull in the discussion. Ikenna returned all of the party's looks, taking a quick glimpse of the children also watching him, and then his eyes rested singularly on the member who knew Ikenna the best, Niyol, who was all too consumed in his bowl of soup.

"Dominus?" someone else in the party spoke up. "Could that be why you sent urgent word for your glass branches of blossoms to be delivered to you, and you have come back without them?"

A subtle stir coursed around the table after the question, and Hinuhinu boldly asked, "Yes, dominus, were the blossoms an offering for a woman?"

Ikenna looked at Hinuhinu, clearing his throat before answering. "The Daichi family was very kind and hospitable to me during my stay. I wanted to give them something of mine, valuable and personal, as a gift."

"And as a gift to a woman, sir?" Niyol quietly pressed, eating more of his soup.

Ikenna eyed him, but when he received no reciprocation of eye contact, he uttered in a low voice, "I suppose you all thought I never would again, as so many years have gone by. It is true that I have been focused mainly on my work and service to the country. I know there are some who think I have been trapped in the past, that that is why I have not..." Ikenna gave his head a nod. "Yes. I gave one of the branches to a woman. A very fine woman, to be sure."

Silence reigned as the party surrounding the table shared looks among themselves, and then Hinuhinu asked aloud, "So then, sir, should we all begin readying the estate for the appearance of a new domina?"

Ikenna's eyes veered to Hinuhinu, and he cleared his throat again. "I would say, at the very least, that you all may want to begin thinking in that direction."

Another stretch of quiet elapsed, and then one of the members at the table started to laugh. Others joined in, and words of anticipation and congratulations made their way down to the head of the table. Ikenna held one hand up, wishing to tell his party not to be premature in their congratulations, that nothing was settled or definite. However, Niyol's gaze came over to meet his, a knowing grin pulling at the corner of the man's mouth, and Ikenna heard himself sigh, thinking ahead to the reply letter he was already planning to send to the State Escritoire. He shook his head, lowering his hand, reasoning that he may as well let his party talk while he saw to it that he would be finished with his homecoming dinner sometime before the next day. He was eager to resume conducting his business affairs.

LETTERS WENT BACK AND forth between Ikenna's estate and the Daichi house over the summer. Ikenna always sent out two letters and received two in return, his intentions growing stronger over the course of the season. In the autumn, he headed out on a trip back to Daichi's village, bringing along Niyol, and among his other items, bringing a dark cedar box. When the men arrived in the village, Niyol secured rooms for them in the community's inn while Ikenna sent a request for a consultation with the village prophet.

The next afternoon, Ikenna was welcomed into the Daichi house by Delmi. Ikenna's eyes instinctively made a swift search for Ahnna, and he had to remind himself that class for her boys and girls would still be in session for the day. As Ikenna followed Delmi through the foreroom, he took a passing look at himself in the great, ornamental mirror on one of the foreroom walls, hoping that his look was sufficiently composed. Delmi led him back to Daichi's alcove, adjacent to the study, where Ikenna was fairly baffled to find Daichi eating.

"Ah. Ikenna, son. Come and sit down," Daichi invited him as Delmi left.

Ikenna came in but did not sit, bowing and holding out the cedar box he had brought. A meeting of this sort would not traditionally permit him to come empty-handed. "Good afternoon, profeta. For you, if you will allow me." He opened the box, taking out a gleaming silver decanter and chalice, each covered with etchings of magnolias, and he set them down on Daichi's table. "I sent for these over the summer. I hope they are to your liking."

Daichi reached out to lift the silver cup, pleasure in his eyes. "Why, my sincere thanks, Ikenna. Fine pieces, they are."

"You are most welcome," Ikenna replied, closing the box, placing it down on the table as well, and remaining on his feet.

"I was happy to receive your request to meet," Daichi told him, motioning across his table. "Do sit down." Ikenna sat then, declining the offer of a slice of Daichi's bread. "I know you did not expect this," Daichi chuckled, "but I have found that by sharing food with even my most nervous visitors, I am usually successful in showing them it is acceptable to breathe, in here." Ikenna smiled briefly but said nothing, and Daichi regarded him with shrewd curiosity. "Well. You have come with the look of one who has a pertinent topic he, at least, *wishes* to speak on."

Ikenna nodded. "That is my wish, sir. But I am fast coming to realize that at such a juncture, words do not seem to readily avail themselves, no matter how well-rehearsed they may have been beforehand."

"Hm." Daichi's head moved up and down as he dipped a piece of his bread into a bowl of sauce, eating the morsel. "I think words forever avail themselves readily. We have but to find them. Even so, you spent days in my house, earlier this year, using no words at all. I did not blame you, knowing for myself what recuperation can take place in a period of silence. But I could tell at the time that, with or without words, you were in no way indifferent to the presence of my Ahnna."

Ikenna ran a hand over his chin. "No, sir, I was not."

"I take it she is the reason why you have requested to speak with me today."

"She is, sir."

Daichi rubbed his fingers together over his bowl. "So. She was out longer than usual, yesterday. You must have found her and covered her with your principal, when you arrived in the village."

"Oh, no. No, sir, I have done no such thing as of yet."

"You have not? Then I must ask what purpose has brought about this visit."

Ikenna shifted his sitting position, slightly. "I know this is not the most usual practice of a suitor, as far as order goes, but I wanted to be completely sure of your view on this matter, before I proceed. You are not just any man, this is not just any family, and I know you think much of Ahnna's respected position as magistra here."

Daichi sat back, folding his hands together. "That is accurate. I am glad that you have given it thought. But, Ahnna will always be a magistra. In whatever station she holds, she will study and instruct, study and instruct. When it is our nature, our destiny, we are what we are wherever we go. And by whatever means we have or choose to manifest ourselves, we inevitably manifest ourselves.

"Even you, Ikenna—even you are a warrior, whether on the field or in business or matters of state. I have heard you lecture on the antiquated restrictions that once hindered our trade, the prohibition to deal with nations being held under centuries-old grudges and prejudices. You are a man who will always find a way to fight for the wellbeing and prosperity of the people you love, and having a woman at your side who is gentle, gracious, and gifted to teach, gifted to clarify ideas, will in no way impair you. To navigate our newfound sovereignty, we need guidance from within. You and Ahnna are ideal ones in the generation to have a hand in providing such guidance, to whatever regions your sphere of influence will extend. You have a good name, and you already have the ear of the very Chief of State, an auspicious detail."

Ikenna was silent, having not counted on receiving such openly favorable words from Daichi.

The older man shrugged, saying, "Being a man of business, you should be about your next order of business quickly, my son. For although Ahnna does not seem to recognize it, you are not the only man around whose attention has been captured by her." Daichi unfolded his hands, sitting back up to his table. "I would tell you to do it right now, but I am sure Ahnna will be difficult to track down after she is finished teaching today. Her mother heard that you were coming and no doubt told Ahnna to busy herself with something unnecessary before returning home, in case you and I would require extra time to have it out about her. But class will be over for the week, and you are more than welcome to come here early tomorrow, to join us for breakfast. You can see Ahnna then, yes?"

Ikenna needed to hear nothing more. "*Yes.*" He rose to his feet, bowing again to Daichi, an uninhibited smile on his face. "My deepest appreciation, sir. You have been most generous." He moved back a few steps before turning from the laughter in Daichi's sagacious eyes. Ikenna would positively make his way back here in the morning, early.

However, even earlier the next morning, before Ikenna showed up, it was intangibly obvious that a portentous shadow had fallen over the Daichi house. When Ahnna joined her mother in the cookery to help prepare breakfast, the older woman whispered with concern, "Your father stayed all night in his alcove. I do not believe he has slept. I got up during the night to check on him, but he was in prayer, so I did not disturb him."

The women had not gotten far into the meal preparation when Daichi showed up at the doorway of the cookery, his broad, glimmering eyes and ashen countenance causing both of the women to stop what they were doing. "Dominus?" Delmi addressed him, taking a step toward him.

Daichi looked at his wife without appearing to fully see her. "Danger is coming," he uttered in a hoarse voice.

Ahnna went a little numb. She wondered if this had anything to do with the meeting she knew her father and Ikenna had had the previous afternoon, while she had stayed behind longer at the school for a second day. She'd wanted to finish scrubbing the floors of the unused theatre. "Danger?"she spoke up. "Where? Here?"

"Here," Daichi answered. "Not to this village, but to the region. I saw the mountains, last night. There was a band of armed men trekking through them. They were planning to attack a community, likely to raid for goods or livestock. I do not believe they had only one village in mind, and they would be looking to add to their numbers."

Delmi had a sharp intake of breath. "Add to their numbers? Who are these men? From where do they come?"

"That has not been made clear to me," Daichi told her. "I must meet with some of the profeti, to learn what they have seen or heard on the matter. It will not be long before the would-be raiders begin their trek."

It was not an abnormal occurrence for Daichi to suddenly call for or to be called to a conference with other prophets in the region, but Ahnna was particularly dismayed to hear this forecasting of danger when they'd had barely a moment to settle into pristine peace. "Oh, Father," she moaned.

"Do not worry, little love." Daichi turned toward Ahnna with his absent gaze. "There is time to stop this. But not much."

Delmi walked over to Daichi then. "A martial brigade will be sent to the mountains to stop them, will it not? But surely you will not go up there on watch. Will it come to that?"

"It cannot come to that," Ahnna interjected. "I hear that the snows started up there earlier than usual, this year. Our medicus has said that you must avoid being out in the cold as much as possible now, Father, correct? Your bones... Moreover, the mountains are more hazardous than the lowland battlefields you stood watch at during the war."

"I will meet with the profeti. We will determine what must be done," Daichi said, and then he blinked, seeming to really look at Delmi now as he reached for her. "Please do not worry, my family," he urged, enclosing Delmi in his arms.

When Ikenna arrived at the Daichi residence that morning, breakfast had been temporarily forgotten and Delmi had gloomily retreated alone to her side room, as the master of the house had already gone. Ahnna welcomed Ikenna into the foreroom and gave him an explanation, completing it with, "I hope he will not go up to the mountains himself. Let the other profeti go, if necessary."

Ikenna examined this troubled maiden before him, wanting to tell her how he'd missed her in the months since he had last seen her. He shook his head at this adverse turn of events. "Well,

I must depart then, if the profeti agree and a brigade is to be assembled."

Ahnna held up her hands. "Ikenna, you will not go with a brigade, will you? Are you not retired from fighting?"

"I do not intend to go up to fight. But I would like to have a hand in the selection of brigaders. I must go to my man Niyol at the inn, so that we can be off at once."

"But...you have only just arrived," Ahnna murmured, knowing her argument to be impractical but feeling driven to make it nonetheless.

Ikenna hesitated for a moment and then stepped forward, taking one of Ahnna's hands into his. "You have wished to see me, then, as much as I have wished to see you?"

"Of course I have. You are my friend. I told you something would be missing here, when you left for home."

Ikenna reached with his free hand, placing a finger under Ahnna's chin. "You know, my home has not been the same either. Something has seemed to be missing there, as well."

Ahnna's brows came closer together. "Oh, dear. Has something happened to one of your people on the estate?"

"What? No." Ikenna's hand lowered from Ahnna's face. "My people are well." He wrestled with the inclination to make himself plain, to proclaim his intentions in full, here and now, but if there was one thing he did not plan to do, he did not plan to rush through paying suit. That deed would have to wait.

He pressed Ahnna's fingers and released them, telling her he would be back to see her as soon as possible. "Do not worry, Ahnna."

One corner of Ahnna's mouth moved dryly upward. "My father told us the same. Sometimes easy to say when you are going off to do something, not having to stay behind to be still and hope. Not that there is anything wrong with being still and hoping, I just—well, I am just going to stop, lest I say something I should not."

Ikenna was weighing the option of embracing Ahnna, wondering how she might react to such a gesture, but Delmi showed up in the foreroom to greet him then. She apologized for her husband's absence and for breakfast not being prepared, asking Ikenna if he would like to stay until the meal was ready. Ikenna thanked Delmi and declined, explaining why he had to take his leave.

Two days later, a messenger boy came to the Daichi house not long after dawn, knocking relentlessly on the door until Ahnna came to answer it.

"Magistra, I was sent to tell the household that raiders are expected in the mountains, men are being sent to stop them, and some of the profeti are going up on watch."

Dread washed the color out of Ahnna's face. "Then my father Daichi has gone up?"

"I believe so, magistra."

The messenger boy had only been gone for a short time when Delmi, after fruitlessly searching through the farmhouse to ask Ahnna who had been at the door, went outside and discovered Ahnna in the stable. She was dressed in a combination of her own and her father's clothing, tying a loaded pack onto a horse.

"Daughter? What are you doing?"

Ahnna finished fastening the pack and led the horse out of its stall. "A messenger boy came by. I am going to get Father. He might be heading to the mountains with the other profeti."

"Ahnna! What on earth...? We hear of danger heading through the mountains, and you plan on riding up there alone to get right in the middle of it yourself?"

"I am not getting into the middle of danger. I am just going to stop Father before he does, before he hurts himself. He will not listen if we send somebody else to get him. He will not like to see me out there, especially alone, and so he will come back with me. We both know he is not in good enough health for this task."

"Yes, we know that!" Delmi made as if to go pull the reins of the horse out of Ahnna's hand. "But your doing this is not the answer, Ahnna. Have you lost your head?"

Ahnna kept a firm hold on the reins, her eyes enlarging. "No, Mother, I have *not* lost my head! This head that has been full of images of blood and pain for three years. Our countrymen coming in wounded or too often dying on Father's floors. You know even better than I do how quickly the times have aged him. He has seen more than enough." Ahnna climbed up onto the horse. "Please go to the school. Tell my boys and girls that there is no class today," she requested over her shoulder as she rode out of the stable, leaving Delmi standing there, bewildered.

Out in the village streets, where news of some disturbance in the mountains was spreading, more than one resident was puzzled to see the schoolmistress flying by on horseback toward the south, with no time to share her usual smiles and greetings.

Chapter Four

IKENNA WAS ALL BUT oblivious to the cold up here. He had not planned on coming into the mountains himself.

Days had gone by. Commissioned brigaders had in fact intercepted a band of armed men headed to ransack a community on another side of the mountains, and the band had been stopped, but not without a cost. While the brigaders had left no would-be raider alive, they had lost nearly a third of their own men. Additionally, the early turn in the weather in the mountains that year meant that the snow was already heavy, and an avalanche had occurred after the fighting, killing some of the remaining men, trapping others. Word was sent down for more help.

Ikenna would not have personally gone, but besides the word for help from the mountains, he'd happened to also receive a letter from the house of Daichi on the same day. It was a short note written in Delmi's hand, saying little more than:

Ahnna went up to find her father, days ago. Neither one has returned home.

So here Ikenna was with others, including Niyol and Hinuhinu, riding through the cold with tools and supplies, headed toward a covered mountain cave.

Ikenna had been filled in on what had supposedly happened here. The prophets hadn't been too close to the fighting, but apparently having heard the oncoming avalanche, they'd backed into a cave to avoid being buried beneath snow and rocks or being forced off of a cliff. Now they remained stuck in the cave. While most of the men were riding on to find the brigaders in need of aid, Ikenna, his present party members, and a few others stopped and dismounted at the site of the cave to start digging away at the frozen snow, rocks, and debris.

Ikenna could no longer be insensible to the cold when entrance into the cave had finally been mined out, as it promptly became evident that those inside had not found anything in that dark, barren trap to make a fire with. While the prophets, generally weak or dazed, were being assisted or carried out of the cave, Ikenna traveled a ways deeper inside with his torch, not wanting to hear what the prophets were reporting to their rescuers in saddened whispers. Niyol followed close behind Ikenna, and they rounded a corner, stopping. Ikenna had hoped that Ahnna might actually have made it somewhere else, or would have even made it back to her home, by the time he'd received Delmi's letter. But his hope vanished like an extinguished flame as he beheld what he had so wished he would not have to see.

Why had Ahnna made the decision to come up here? And why, for the love of all things sane and rational, had she not stayed close to the others in the cave to await a rescue? Or had she been with the others for a while but had been compelled to break off from them to handle her burden alone? For there Ahnna was on the ground, huddled against a cave wall, her arms cradling the upper half of her father.

It took hardly a second for Ikenna to realize that Daichi's cradled body, as the prophets had whispered, was indeed only a body, now.

Upon seeing the light of the torch, Ahnna's eyes came up, not even squinting at the sudden brightness as she looked to Ikenna. Her mouth moved, a grating sound coming from her throat while her neglected voice tried to function. She eventually let out a choked, "'Kenna...help," as Ikenna handed the torch to Niyol and made his way over to kneel in front of her.

Ahnna's jaw trembled. Her hair, loose and stringy with the cold, shook as a shudder coursed through her body, and her teeth chattered together as Ikenna's hands came toward her. Yet, before Ikenna could touch her, Ahnna hoarsely, desperately pleaded, "*Help* him."

Ikenna stared at her, and then he let his eyes lower to the stiff body in Ahnna's arms. Full of anguish, he reasserted to himself that what had been Daichi was beyond help. Despite herself, Ahnna must have been quite aware of this, because when Ikenna's hands latched onto the corpse to relieve her of it, she did not attempt to slacken her grip. Ikenna looked into Ahnna's stricken gaze while he tugged at Daichi's body. "Ahnna. Dear Ahnna, please. Let him go."

Ahnna's face twitched, another tremor running through her as she gaped at Ikenna, not obeying him. Ikenna tugged a second time, his shaking voice calm, but adamant. "Please, Ahnna. It is time to leave. Your father has already. You must let him go."

A seemingly infinite moment passed before Ahnna shifted, and though no sign of acquiescence showed in her eyes, Ikenna accepted her slight movement as her surrender. Ikenna pulled, and Ahnna's rigid arms loosened enough to allow Daichi's body to be taken away from her. Watching Ahnna's fixed, unnatural stare, Ikenna motioned Niyol over with his head. "Give me the torch. Carry her for me. Be careful—she is freezing."

Ikenna knew his last instruction was unnecessary, but he said it aloud more for Ahnna's sake than Niyol's. It took more than bodily strength for Ikenna to hoist up that precious dead weight to carry over his shoulder as he led the way back around the corner and out of the cave.

The following days in Daichi's village were quiet ones. The prophet's burial was a simple affair, though many from the area came to pay homage and to witness the gathered prophets' public promotion of Daichi's successor. Delmi attended only part of the ceremony prior to being escorted by mourning villagers back to her farmhouse, and Ahnna could not attend the burial at all, as she had not yet recovered from her freezing confinement in the cave.

An interim schoolmaster had been put on duty for the village children. Ikenna was again staying at the Daichi house, insisting on performing chores with the farmhands, sitting by as a support while a grieving Delmi received visits from compassionate friends, and taking a part of Ahnna's care into his own hands. He made sure never to be in the way while Delmi tended to her daughter or during the doctor's visits, although the doctor did bring him aside with Delmi one afternoon to explain what he'd concluded had happened to his longtime comrade.

"I just do not think he could handle frigid conditions outdoors anymore, not for that length of time," the doctor lamented, his head sorrowfully moving from side to side. "The other profeti say they did their best to warm him, but it is rather clear that his body, nevertheless, went into shock. Ahnna...pulled him off by herself, to be alone with him, after..."

Ikenna's eyes painfully closed. An image of Ahnna distraughtly dragging her father's lifeless body through a dark cave passed through his mind. He went to sit beside her pallet that evening, watching her in slumber. Her body had to be kept bundled most of the time, her fingers and toes regularly needing to be bathed in water with medicinal solutions to relieve her of the biting effects of the cold. Ikenna would feed her and rub salve into her healing hands and feet, speaking to her much of the time, even though she wouldn't say anything back.

Yet, one morning after Delmi left Ahnna's room and Ikenna came in, the angst that had frozen within Ahnna while she'd sat in that cave with her father seemed to thaw all at once. Delmi rushed back in to help console her while Ikenna had to physically hold Ahnna down, listening to the violent sobs that threatened to rip through her frame. After that gushing current of grief ran its course, Ahnna went limp on her pallet, and Ikenna and Delmi stepped out of the room, assuming that Ahnna was asleep. But she actually heard Ikenna's and Delmi's voices as they headed toward the foreroom.

"I wish I could have asked them, before they were stopped in the mountains, just precisely what they meant by such foolishness," Ikenna passionately hissed.

"I thought they meant revenge," Delmi murmured in weary response. "Revenge for our having won our independence from them."

"No, no, domina, they were not men sent from the enemy empire. They were a rebellious band of our own countrymen."

"What? Our own countrymen? That cannot be true."

"It *should* not be true. Imbecilic hotheads—what was their rationale? To begin destroying this recuperating nation from within, right after we have fought off a vicious adversary? The profeti say the band's intent was to add to their numbers. Could they truly have been looking to take over villages for themselves, to set up their own false rule or maverick distinction of some sort? Are there others around, harboring that diseased frame of mind? This nation must be united for our betterment. We need discipline, to learn corporate and individual restraint. How can a man join with others in constructive thought of the common good and national sovereignty, or of eminence, when he has not yet learned to worthily govern himself?"

Scarcely noticed tears were streaming from Ahnna's tired eyes and soaking into her pillow, and she heard Ikenna go on speaking to collect himself. "Forgive me, domina. My words are insensitively timed. Your house does not need my anger now. I know what it is to lose a spouse, but I also know that my past loss differs from yours in many ways. I only wish to be of continued service to this household for a time, to honor a great man I was privileged to engage with personally, for what seems to have been but a moment."

Delmi's quiet voice was thick with bridled emotion. "Bless you, Ikenna. I am not offended. God help me with my own anger, and other sentiments I am sometimes afraid to name, when I wake up these mornings and my Daichi is not there. I have been glad for your presence and help here, particularly for my daughter's sake. That is, whatever 'glad' can be, for the time being."

Their voices retreated, and Ahnna heard no more, blinking heavily and drifting off to sleep.

When Ikenna went in later that day with food for Ahnna, he was surprised to see her already sitting up against her wall in her blankets, staring toward the window. She looked at Ikenna as he entered the room, her eyes still tired and her voice small and uneven as she spoke to him for the first time since the day of her rescue. "You have been going out of your way for me, sir."

Ikenna walked over to her, kneeling to the floor and setting the food tray down, picking up a bowl of soup. "You did the same for me after Mtihani."

Ahnna allowed him to spoon some soup into her before she pointed out, "I am sure your business needs you, though."

"Niyol has been an exceptional help while I have been away. He and Hinuhinu. They have been traveling between our villages as I have needed them to. I am managing just fine. For now, this is where I should be." He raised another spoonful of soup to Ahnna's mouth, lowering the spoon when she did not take it.

Ahnna's head leaned back against the wall as she inhaled, letting her breath out tremulously. "I have always believed my father to be a wise man, Ikenna." Her head rolled back and forth along the wall. "I could not understand why he would not come with me, when I rode up to get him."

Ikenna watched Ahnna's eyes redden as she went on. "Just because the coming danger had been revealed to him did not mean that he had to go up there himself. It did not mean that the other profeti had to let him. They could see his body failing him as clearly as anyone could. Still, my father insisted on going. He would not come with me, and I would not leave him. But he…" Ahnna's words broke off, and then she resumed in a whisper. "He was the one who saw the cave. The other profeti did not. I did not. We all heard the rumbling, but he was the one who saw the cave and shouted for us all to get inside. If he had not been there, all of the profeti who had gone to the mountains on watch would have died in that avalanche."

Ikenna's hands reflexively tightened around the bowl in his hands. "My God."

Ahnna brought her head up from the wall. "I know it was not the first time it happened, but it was my first time seeing it. Seeing my father save people's lives. Not that he did not save my own life, in a way, when he took me from that orphanage. And here he was obliged to save me again, when I was the one who proved to be unwise, by going up into those mountains."

Ikenna distractedly stirred the bowl of soup. "So." His head nodded in thought. "He did know what he was doing."

Ahnna only sat there for a while, and then she brought one hand from underneath her blankets. "He did. And you are right." Holding Ikenna's eyes, she lifted her hand to his face, placing her palm alongside his cheek. "He was a great man. It is fitting that you would want to be here to honor him."

Ikenna nodded another time. "One reason for my being here, yes."

"One reason? Then the most important, I am sure."

"All of my reasons are important." Ikenna had a mind to turn his face toward Ahnna's hand, that he might press his lips into her palm, but considering that such an action might somehow upset the serenity between them, he said, without moving, "You must know that I am growing to love you, Ahnna."

Ahnna's amazement was visible. "Are you?"

"Absolutely. Cannot you tell?" Ikenna asked, his pulse hastening as Ahnna's thumb ponderingly stroked his lightly bearded cheek, the tips of her other fingers going up to caress his temple.

Ahnna's head went faintly up and down, her fingers withdrawing from Ikenna's face. "It appears that my hands are feeling a little better," she told him, glancing down at the bowl of soup.

Ikenna raised the bowl, thinking that Ahnna aimed to take it from him, but when she merely lifted the spoon, Ikenna leaned toward her, holding the bowl for her as she began to feed herself.

Ikenna wanted to tell Ahnna that Niyol and Hinuhinu had come by the Daichi house on a matter of business the day before, while Ahnna had been sleeping. Hinuhinu had pointed out a portrait that Ahnna had painted of herself, hanging on a wall of the entryway. Niyol had stared approvingly at it, saying nothing, but Hinuhinu commented to Ikenna, "If she paints as accurately as the woman in the picture is pleasing to the eye, it is no wonder you have not brought her to visit the estate, that you have kept her all to yourself. No impertinence meant, dominus."

Nevertheless, Ikenna chose not to share that bit of news with Ahnna. For the moment, he was certain he had let her know enough.

OVER THE NEXT STRING of days, Ahnna made steady progress in her recovery. On an evening when she was finally well enough to come to the supper table, Delmi sat watching her daughter eat, and then she looked to Ikenna, waiting until she caught his eyes. Delmi's gaze flitted over to Ahnna and back, and Ikenna returned Delmi's look, taking a while to understand. He was staggered at the woman's boldness, he himself feeling that it was rather soon after Daichi's death for this. Yet, perhaps that was part of what was impelling Delmi, who knew what her husband's wishes had been and who'd also been intimately reminded, by his passing, of the limitedness of time, of life.

Ikenna took in a subtle breath. He had imagined taking Ahnna out into nature, out into the peaceful, amber colors of autumn for it, but she was not yet fit for any long walks out of doors. All the same, if the mistress of the house had spoken, albeit without speaking, then it behooved him to make haste.

The next day, Hsiu Mei made a visit to the Daichi house to see her friend, bringing along a gift of a lilac day robe. "I remember how gloomy it was around my house when my grandmother died. I thought having something new and lovely might lift your spirits," Hsiu Mei stated, standing with Ahnna in front of the ornamental mirror in the foreroom as Ahnna held the robe up against herself. "Put it on."

"Thank you so much. What elegant taste," Ahnna replied, removing her current robe, being sure not to let the folded piece of parchment discreetly tucked inside fall out, and she tried on her new robe over her dress. Ahnna walked a ways before the mirror, girlishly posing.

Hsiu Mei laughed. "My goodness, Ahnna, what will we ever do with that walk of yours? Such definition in every step."

Ahnna smiled. "Why must you always critique the way I walk? This—" Ahnna began, trip-tripping across the floor in her best exaggerated impression of Hsiu Mei's gait, "—is walking as if you are eternally skimming hot coals." Ahnna made her way back over to the mirror in her usual stride, only a trace of variation in her step showing that she had not been well for weeks. "This way flows better."

"But your hips. It draws such attention to your hips."

"What is wrong with that? Everyone has hips. They are nothing for a girl to be ashamed of."

Hsiu Mei moved behind Ahnna as both women faced the mirror, and Hsiu Mei pointed down to the skirt of Ahnna's robe. "It makes your dresses and robes swish around so. That draws even more attention to the fact that you do not tie your sashes correctly."

"Oh, my sashes! Forever and again with my sashes," Ahnna groaned, untying the article around her waist. "What is so horribly incorrect about the way I tie them?"

"Let me show you." Hsiu Mei reached to tie Ahnna's sash in Ahnna-fashion, but she discovered that she did not know Ahnna's technique. The two women found themselves laughing as Hsiu Mei struggled in her demonstration, so neither one of them was aware that Ikenna had come into the room.

He moved so soundlessly that the women remained ignorant of his presence until he spoke up. "Perhaps, Hsiu Mei, you will allow me."

The laughing in the foreroom came to an abrupt halt. Hsiu Mei's and Ahnna's heads came up, startled, Hsiu Mei letting go of Ahnna's sash and whipping around. "Sir," she greeted Ikenna, stepping aside.

Ahnna did not turn around, watching alertly through the mirror as Ikenna took Hsiu Mei's place behind her. The room itself seemed to go still along with the three of them, but when Ikenna took an end of Ahnna's sash into each of his hands, bringing them both around Ahnna to tie them, Hsiu Mei bowed her head in a rush. She kept her head down as she silently backed herself to a remote corner of the room.

Ahnna stared into the glass as Ikenna tied her sash in a way she had never tied it before. He adjusted her skirt with a few light tugs. "I was taught to be meticulous about clothing from the onset of my military training. Everything there has to be precise, so I picked up on much. You see? This is the way my mother would secure her sashes. It was different, although she was a very strict and traditional woman, in many respects."

"Ah." Ahnna inspected her robe in the mirror, cautiously swallowing. "An interesting style."

"I agree. And no one minded its differentness, as I recall." Ikenna took the knot of the sash in one hand, undoing it in one smooth motion. Ahnna's mouth fell open as her robe did, but no words would come as Ikenna eased closer to her, his chest settling against her back.

Ahnna's eyes dropped from the mirror as Ikenna's hands each took hold of the opposite sides of her robe, wrapping them about her. With his right hand holding the robe against her, he took up the sash with his left, beginning to tie it as Ahnna would, saying to her, "I have yet to see you in formal attire, but this is the way you customarily go about fastening your everyday sashes." He turned his head, bringing his lips near to her ear. "All the better for me to like it for its being different, yes?"

The breath he used to pose the question brushed across Ahnna's earlobe and floated down her neck. When her heart skipped, she tipped her head to one side in an effort to veer her ear away from Ikenna's mouth. Yet, her doing so only left her neck more noticeably exposed, and Ikenna brought his face in nearer to it, beginning to hum a familiar tune while he finished tying the sash. To Ahnna's wonderment, Ikenna commenced to softly sing a version of the song with his own words.

> *Hawks and geese may not get so far by walking*
> *and a horse or tiger might lose ground with a crawl*
> *but how far my soul leapt just while she was talking*
> *and desire deepened when she used no words at all.*

Ikenna untied the knot again so that the sash wouldn't be in the way, his arms lingering around Ahnna while he tenderly ran the tip of his nose along her throat, inhaling her scent, rendering her significantly warm and short of breath. Eventually, he pulled his arms back until his hands rested on either side of Ahnna's waist. Then, with one hand still in place, he brought his other to the front of his principal, untying it.

On account of his closeness, Ahnna could sense his movements, and when his remaining hand lifted from her waist, she knew that his principal was being removed.

Ahnna's arms hung stiffly at her sides. When she felt the fabric of Ikenna's principal graze at her elbows, she compliantly straightened them, allowing Ikenna to slip the sleeves over her hands and arms and to slide the robe up over her shoulders.

Ahnna did not raise her eyes any higher than Ikenna's shirt as he came around to face her. He took the front of his principal, starting to wrap one side over the other, but it wasn't until his motions came to a standstill that Ahnna's gaze came up. She saw that he was studying her keenly, a shade of doubt in his stare, and Ahnna swallowed a second time, asking him, "Why do you hesitate?"

His answer was unhurried, pensive. "Because you do."

Ahnna's voice almost caught on her next words. "But I thought you love me."

"I do love you," Ikenna affirmed, ardency deepening his tone.

"Then why do you hesitate?"

Looking Ahnna over, Ikenna told her, "I am not sure if your acceptance here is one of favor, or if it is merely resigned."

Ahnna looked downward again, her words barely audible. "Neither am I sure. I should have anticipated this more deliberately." She turned, causing Ikenna to release his grip on his principal. With her back to him, Ahnna rolled her shoulders backward to make the robe slip, and when she felt Ikenna take hold of the garment, she let it fall down her arms and come off of her.

Holding her day robe closed against her, not bothering with her sash anymore, she walked away from Ikenna, picking up the older robe she'd removed and leaving the foreroom. It was not long before the door of her side room was heard down the hallway, sliding to a close, and Ikenna was left standing there, his discarded principal in his hands.

He did not speak, did not move for a moment. The weight of the light fabric of his robe seemed to increase the longer he remained there, and then his legs leadenly went into motion as he too left the room.

Hearing the sound of the front door of the farmhouse opening and closing with Ikenna's departure, Hsiu Mei raised her head in shock, gaping into the empty foreroom.

Chapter Five

"SO YOU ARE LEAVING then, sir?"

"In the morning, yes. I wished to stay until Ahnna recovered. She is much better now. She will soon be resuming her duties as magistra. You and Daichi's farmhands will have everything settled for the winter shortly. And the people of this village respect you and are determined to look after you, I have observed. There is no longer any reason for me to stay."

"No reason at all?"

Ikenna watched as Delmi's brows rose, and he shook his head. "I do not wish to sound ungrateful in any way. I have greatly appreciated your hospitality, and I hope I might go forward in a manner that will do justice to my having known your husband, much as I wish to perpetually honor the memory of my own parents." Ikenna took a glance around the alcove he was standing in this evening, where he'd found Delmi sitting at Daichi's table, polishing the wood. "I am only saying that I no longer have any real reason not to return to my responsibilities at home. I have been away so much, even after the war. I must get back to lecturing as well, on more than trade. We cannot let any residual embers from those rebels in the mountains spark into flame anywhere else. If embers of revolt exist within our borders, we must snuff them out."

"Yes, yes, of course. That must be seen to," Delmi replied with a nod. "But I must speak plainly with you, Ikenna, sir. Perhaps my idea of the timing may seem hasty to you, given that the earth of her father's grave has had only weeks to chill. Then she was not well, but it does seem to me that you would have paid suit to my daughter by now."

"Yes. Well." Ikenna cleared his throat. "Permit me to own to you that I have been weighed down with the impression that your daughter must feel I am too old of a man for her."

Delmi dismissed his comment with a toss of her hand. "Oh, why would you say such a thing? Ahnna feels nothing of the sort. She is not a child, and you are far from being an old man."

"Thank you. But you must understand, domina, that your daughter—she has already rejected my suit. I approached her earlier today, while Hsiu Mei was here."

Delmi appeared to be stunned by that clarification, but only for a second. "Dear me. That would explain why the girls were so quiet at dinner, and why you did not join us then, nor for supper. I assumed you were out on business." Ikenna said nothing to that, and Delmi shook her head. "There is no sense in Ahnna's doing something like this. Notwithstanding the mild surface the two of you tend to keep as a protective casing over your friendship, I have still seen the mutual esteem, care, and attraction between you. And she has proven herself to be an excellent nurse in general, but considering all of the concern she showed you while you were not in health, if you think Ahnna showed that same degree for every soldier the war brought here for help, you are mistaken. Daichi and I have hosted many people in this house, our family has been active in this community and beyond, and I have never seen a man who has had the effect on my Ahnna that you have on her. She adores you, sir."

Ikenna was thoroughly taken aback. When he persisted not to speak, Delmi laughed delicately, looking down at Daichi's table, running wistful fingertips over it. "Ikenna, please bear in mind that fear and love cannot operate together for long. If there is something that Ahnna fears, I would suggest that you get to the root of the issue." Delmi looked back up, taking the cloth she had been polishing the table with and rising to her feet. "I speak for both my husband and myself when I say that you and Ahnna quite belong with each other. So you must gather your bearings, sir, and pay suit to her again. You already have the blessing of her father, and of her mother."

Ikenna beheld the woman before him, not without some incredulity, and she smiled at him before stepping from behind the table and making her way out of the alcove. Ikenna stood there for minutes after she was gone, wondering at the sound of the small additional laugh Delmi had left him with.

Ikenna did return to his own village the next morning while his thoughts moved a ways ahead of him in feverish planning. Overnight, as he'd reflected on Delmi's words, he'd decided that he was going to take a considerable risk, and he would need help from a number of people to do it.

That week, Ahnna obtained permission from the doctor and her mother to spend a short time outdoors, and she donned a hooded cloak, going out to the Daichi fields on an afternoon. Walking over the grounds where the crops had been harvested, she lifted her face to the sky, drawing a breath from the autumn wind, missing her father. Her thoughts then unavoidably traveled to the heated discussion she'd had with Hsiu Mei on the day of her visit, after Ikenna had left the house with his principal in his hands.

"What on earth do you mean by refusing him that way, Ahnna?" Hsiu Mei had demanded when she entered Ahnna's side room, finding her friend standing at the window, looking out. "What was the problem? Did you not like the way he went about it?"

Ahnna had still been holding her robe closed against her with folded arms. "I was not ready. I have never been—he has never touched me that way before. There was fire in his hands, I think." Ahnna's head tipped against the window. "Or maybe the fire was in me. Now I do not know."

"Fire, fire indeed! Under a boiling pot. There was more steam in that room than over a thousand bubbling washtubs. I was certain I would soon have to leave you two alone, for all of that. So you did not like how he did it?"

"Of course I liked it. I could have fainted clean away. He was beautiful about it. It would only have been more wonderful if he could have finished all that he meant to do."

"What? Then, ready or unready, how could you refuse the man? How could you pass up this opportunity? It is more than plain that you long for him. I could see it when you first introduced me to him in the spring. What is more, you have been corresponding with him all this time. Have you been giving him false hope?"

Ahnna raised her head and spun around from the window. "Oh, how *could* I resist him, resist corresponding with him?

Would you that I had lost the friendship he and I started when he was brought here? I value having it."

"Right. You value his friendship," Hsiu Mei had remarked with somewhat of a grunt. "And you *want* him, Ahnna. You care for him."

"I certainly do," Ahnna answered, unfolding her arms. "Is it so impossible to care enough for a man not to let him marry you?"

"I beg your pardon? Why would you not want Ikenna to marry you?"

"You know the situation regarding my birth, Hsiu Mei."

"Yes, but who cares about that? My teasing aside and in all seriousness, who gives it a thought? Did I hear incorrectly or misunderstand, or did he not just mention how he likes your being different?"

"He was referring more to individuality than to nationality."

"What of it? You told him before where you are from, did you not? He already knows, and he does not care."

"Yes I told him where I am from, but I did not specifically tell him that my natural parents were not married."

Hsiu Mei paused, taken off guard by this information. "Oh." She then shook her head. "Well, you were...you are Daichi's. Daichi and Delmi's. Whatever unfortunate circumstance that may have come before that would not make so much of a difference to Ikenna."

Ahnna spread out her hands. "I am thinking of Ikenna, and more than Ikenna. With the very Chief of State's eyes upon him, he is in position to have more of a voice in this country than he has ever had. He may even be appointed to a national post one day. And not everyone in the entire nation will be so accepting as the people who have personally known Daichi and Delmi have been. Do you really think it would bode well for Ikenna if any opponents of his or anyone looking to defame him chose to use this against him? They would bellow the news abroad that Ikenna is bringing forth children of mixed, even tainted, blood—the blood of his foreign wife, a native of our archenemy. They would say she is originally of an illegitimate spawning, to make it worse."

Hsiu Mei had not had an immediate response for that, so Ahnna had gone on to say, "You may be right. I may have given Ikenna false hope when it was not my wish to, in my attempt not to lose him altogether. And my origins may not matter so much if I am ever to marry a farmer or a woodworker, someone I have grown up with around here. But I cannot risk one day being a stain upon the wide and venerated reputation of a man like Ikenna, being a hazard to his voice. No matter how I have come to love..."

The wind out here in the fields was picking up. Ahnna involuntarily recalled the feel of Ikenna's arms around her, the resonance of his soft humming near her neck. She pulled off the hood of her cloak to allow her disconcerted head to catch the full benefit of the blowing air, as if to sweep away her flustered thoughts.

She stopped walking, closing her eyes. She missed her father. She pressed a hand to the front of her cloak, making sure she could still feel the piece of folded parchment that she had been tucking into her robes and dresses nearly every day for months. What was it that Ikenna had said to her mother the other morning, after Ahnna had broken out in agonized grief over Daichi? If a man would be useful for the common good of everyone, wasn't it necessary for him to learn to worthily govern himself?

Daichi had possessed that kind of ethic, even in his final years. All through the war, he'd put the needs of his people before the demands of his body. Ahnna did not know whether Daichi had been aware that he would not come back from the mountains alive if he went up, but he'd gone to do what he had devoted his life to. He hadn't allowed dread, his or anyone else's, to hinder him. In that way, love had ultimately taken precedence in his life.

Ahnna opened her eyes. Slowly pulling her hood back on, she turned toward the farmhouse, resuming her walk. She had permitted the fear of losing Ikenna to keep her from letting him know sooner that she wasn't at liberty to accept a suit from him. Had she exercised better rule over herself, over her dread, she would have saved him, and his heart, a good amount of trouble.

Ikenna now deserved, at the least, an explanation from her. She preferred not to write one in a letter, as she didn't want to appear as if she wished not to face him, but she would find a way to talk to him about this soon.

Chapter Six

NOT MANY DAYS LATER, it was time for Ahnna to return to her place as schoolmistress. Eager to see her pupils, she bounded up from her pallet early in the morning, but she was startled when Delmi suddenly burst through the door of her room.

"Ahnna, my darling daughter! You are awake at last," Delmi rejoiced.

"At last?" Ahnna glanced out of her window and laughed. "I am up earlier than usual. The sun has barely had time to show its face. What is the rush?"

Delmi hurried over, grabbing up a shawl to throw around Ahnna's shoulders. "Quickly, quickly. I have hot bathwater waiting for you. Then put on a bathrobe and come to breakfast. I will have it ready soon."

Through her bath and breakfast, Ahnna gave into her mother's excitement without asking any questions, but when Delmi would not allow her to tie her hair back into a chignon, Ahnna's curiosity was piqued. "What do you mean I should not pull my hair back?"

"Well, we can plait some over the front as a crown, but the rest should hang free. What are you going to wear? How about your pale yellow dress and day robe with the orange flowers?"

"I typically reserve those for spring. And they are a bit formal for class, are they not? Mother, what is going on?"

"What is going on?" Delmi repeated, a glisten seeping into her eyes. "Must you ask? It will be your first day back as magistra, after you went to the mountains. You...you could have died up there, Ahnna. I could have been left here without my only child, as well as without my husband." Delmi's voice had lowered on her last words, and she rapidly blinked, smiling. "Your children will be overjoyed to see you, and I am proud of you. Please, cannot we treat this as the special day it is?"

Ahnna smiled at Delmi as well, having to blink back dampness in her own eyes at the sight of her mother's emotion. "It is a special day. Thank you. You are right."

Later, after her mother had wished her a good day in class and had seen her out of the house, Ahnna started off walking slower than usual. She was ahead of her normal time and was wearing some of her nicest clothing beneath her cape. However, when she reached the crest of the hill to the west, she was surprised to see a group of her pupils there, waiting for her.

"Magistra!"

"Well! Good morning," Ahnna greeted the boys and girls as they dashed toward her. "You children are up and on your way to the school before me? Have I mistakenly overslept?"

"No, no," one of the boys answered, coming to take Ahnna's books out of her hands, stacking them with his own books. "I will carry these for you. We must hurry!"

"Yes!" one of the girls piped up, taking Ahnna's right hand while another girl took her left. "Class is a bore when you are gone."

The spirited group journeyed on through the village streets in the direction of the school, Ahnna smiling and addressing familiar faces as they went by. Once she and the children had passed the lake, she was perplexed to hear and see them coming upon a number of horses hitched outside of the schoolhouse. "What is this? Visitors must be here, unannounced. A crowd of them. But, so early?" Ahnna mused, making to head toward the horses and schoolhouse, but the girls pulled at her hands.

"No, this way, magistra. To the theatre."

"The theatre? But we are going to class, children," Ahnna told her pupils. They did not hear her over their sudden din of noise, as they were shouting toward the theatre building.

"*She is here!*"

When Ahnna looked to the theatre, she halted. The rest of her pupils came streaming out of the building to welcome her, and a delighted greeting for all of them came to Ahnna's lips. She was not to issue the greeting, however, as she noticed with puzzlement that some of the messenger boys from her class were not dressed for school but were wearing their blue uniforms.

Next, a cluster of other villagers came out of the theatre as well. Three among them were Hsiu Mei, the village doctor, and Daichi's recently promoted successor. With him were some of the prophets from other villages who'd been in the cave with Ahnna and her father in the mountains. Ahnna was about to ask them what was happening, but a line of other men and women came flowing out of the theatre. Ahnna did not yet know that there before her was nearly every member of the party from

Ikenna's estate, being led out by Niyol, the only one she recognized.

The children were engrossed in lively chatter, some of them jumping around, and Hsiu Mei and the maidens with her were busy laughing at the look on Ahnna's face. Hence, she had no chance to present them with any coherent questions before she heard the pounding of hooves behind her. Ahnna turned around, her hand coming up to her mouth in astonishment when she realized that it was Ikenna riding up on horseback, wearing a rather elaborate cloak, and her mother was up on the horse with him.

"Ah! Noble magistra," Ikenna called out as soon as he was close enough, and Niyol came forward as the horse was brought to a stop. Ikenna dismounted and stepped away, leaving Niyol to assist a glowing Delmi off of the horse while Ikenna moved toward Ahnna, saying, "How lovely to see you. Behind me is Niyol. You might remember being helped by him in the mountains. Over there is Hinuhinu and the rest of my party, save a few members who stayed behind to mind the estate and the little ones there. I will be glad to introduce each one to you, when the occasion allows.

"Now, magistra, you know that I am partial to the theatre, and you are right on time for a production, the inaugural one for this establishment, I understand. No, no—there is no need to look so anxious. You will not have to direct or otherwise take charge of this production. You have only to be in it, and to be yourself." Ikenna gave Ahnna a low bow, and with that, her enthusiastic pupils tugged at her, leading her to enter the theatre building.

Once inside, one of the boys took Ahnna's cape for her. She was ushered to the front of the theatre to ascend the stage while the assorted audience of villagers, prophets, and party members swarmed in to stand and observe. Ahnna stood nervously alone on the stage until Ikenna entered onto the platform through a side door, having removed his cloak to reveal a striking black principal trimmed with gold. Ahnna saw that his black trousers also had gold trim, and she thought she had never seen Ikenna look more handsome, or more in earnest.

Ikenna walked toward her and stood holding a hand out to their audience. "I owe much thanks to each person here," he declared in everyone's hearing, "particularly to Delmi and Hsiu Mei, who assisted me and my party in making sure the right aggregation of people would be present. I also wished to see to it that messenger boys would be on hand to herald what I sincerely hope will be good news in the village square immediately following this production, if they may be excused from class for a time to do so."

Ikenna lowered his arm, turning more fully toward Ahnna, saying, "It may be an unconventional order of action, but I thought it important to convey to you, tangibly and symbolically, magistra..." His voice softened. "Ahnna. I thought it important to convey to you publicly that you are a most admired and honored woman, and you have the support of many people with you. With backing such as this, you need never be fretful. That is, afraid. You are not alone. You do not have to face any day or difficulty alone. You are safe."

Hearing that, Ahnna could not help but to recollect the first time she'd striven to comfort a wounded Ikenna after one of his nightmares. His eyes never wavered from her face as he said, "You undoubtedly know what I am about this morning, dear Ahnna, so feel free to express any reason you believe why I should not be about this very thing. Or, if that would not please you, then you need not speak on the matter, we need not revisit this again, and not a soul in the room will honor you less. I will still count it a privilege to know you and to serve you by any means that I can, going forward, as your devoted and grateful friend, whatever your response today may be." Ikenna ended there with a nod to indicate that he had stated his piece.

Ahnna could only guess at what sentiments and unspoken questions Ikenna's words might have aroused in the room. It was likely that the majority of the onlookers in the theatre did not know that this regional tradesman had paid suit to this village schoolmistress once already, and had been rejected. Now here he was, calculatedly risking another refusal, in the presence of his and her people, in an endeavor to plainly, imaginatively communicate his unbroken regard and desire for her. "Oh, Ikenna," Ahnna heard herself say.

She stopped, having not meant to speak aloud yet. Nonetheless, as this peaceable chance for her to offer Ikenna an explanation in person had been given to her, unanticipated, she chose to keep going, her heart in her throat. "You overwhelm me, sir. I count myself to be the privileged one, and if I am at all admired and honored, you might be more so. It is this very honor of yours that I aim to consider.

"Though I do not presume to foretell the future, I do have a picture of where you will be going, in all probability. You have much work to do, and there are and will be many eyes upon you." Ahnna took the eyes and ears in the room now into account, especially the youngest ones, and she chose her words with discretion. "I once told you about a man and woman who traveled through a country in a caravan, if you remember. Well, that man and woman...were not espoused. And there may be numerous individuals who will one day deem that to be a most unfortunate detail, if it is ever to concern you."

Ahnna watched as Ikenna absorbed and silently interpreted her admission. His eyebrows drew toward one another. "So, in light of that detail," he reflected, "you are unsure about what people may think or may say to slander me, or to discount my legacy?"

Ahnna, in spite of her doubts over the situation, was relieved that he understood. "Precisely."

Ikenna nodded, murmuring, "I see." Then, stepping closer to Ahnna, he projected his voice once more for everyone. "It is true that we can learn much about a person through his country, as well as his parentage. And no one, in his infancy, is given the opportunity to select either. A man is, however, left with the choice of whether or not he will live respectably in the time he has been given.

"Not long ago, a wise man told me that we are who we are, and by whatever means we have or choose to manifest ourselves, we inevitably manifest ourselves. I have also heard that from the time you were very young, you—someone's 'little love'—have graciously manifested yourself, and your destiny."

Ahnna felt her eyes smarting in reaction to that, and she bit her lip to keep it from trembling as Ikenna went on. "I believe you to be someone who has chosen to live and to do well with what you have been given, as have I. But we cannot carry that choice out to the utmost if we spend our lives hiding from what people might think or say one day. Slanderers lose their relevance the more we are focused on the people we have purposed to help." Ikenna reached to take Ahnna's hand into his, whispering, "My Ahnna, you will never have to worry about my honor if you, with all of your grace, will help me to increase it."

The tingle had not left Ahnna's moist eyes, and wanting to give those eyes a moment away from everyone's scrutiny, Ahnna removed her hand from Ikenna's and took hold of his arm, turning her face away from the audience as she moved to place her head against Ikenna's shoulder. She stood there, taking her time to compose herself and to let his words sink in, feeling Ikenna's free hand come up to run along the back of her hair. She thought to ask just once if Ikenna was absolutely sure, but she knew in an instant that she didn't have to, being certain that he would not have expressed such confidence pertaining to the future if he was not sufficiently sure. Her own free hand came up near her heart, pressing to feel the folded parchment tucked in the bodice of her dress as she came to a resolution. She tilted her face up toward Ikenna's ear so that only he would hear her say, "Then, there is no place I would rather fulfill my destiny than alongside you, beloved Ikenna." And she felt him release a long breath before he loosened the sash of her day robe to keep it out of the way.

Ahnna let go of Ikenna's arm so that he could back away enough to remove his principal. He turned a beaming face to the audience of lowering heads as he did so. "Now listen here, children! Your magistra will be wearing a fine robe of mine all day, and you are not free to yank it, to step on its hem, or to spill or smear anything on it. Any offender will be sentenced to sixty uninterrupted minutes of listening to your noble magistra deliver renditions of her favorite folksongs after class. Is that understood?"

Ahnna laughed outright as Ikenna covered her with his principal, and a boisterous ovation ensued from the audience once they'd lifted their heads. Ahnna was wiping at her eyes with her fingers, and Ikenna stood tying his principal's sash into an extravagant knot. "You would think this was a festival or a marriage ceremony itself," Ahnna told him beneath the applause and cheers, indicating the audience with her head.

Ikenna grinned at her, finishing the knot. "They have every reason to celebrate. This production is splendid, is it not? Though it will pale in comparison to the marriage ceremony. Half of the government will pine for an invitation to it when they find out that the Chief of State means to be in attendance."

"What?" Ahnna uttered after a gasp, but Ikenna didn't hear her as he was now urging her to join with him in a sweeping bow to their audience. He then shooed the messenger boys out of the theatre.

"To the village square with you. And make haste! I expect you all to be back for class as soon as possible, and your magistra will report it to me if you are not."

The remainder of the morning blew past Ahnna like a vast, brisk cloud. Later on, she would vaguely remember receiving embraces from her mother and Hsiu Mei and well-wishes from the prophets and the village doctor outside of the theatre. Niyol and the party members all declared their congratulations to the prospective estate mistress prior to mounting their horses and flying off for the trip back to their village. The final two to leave Ahnna and her pupils there were Ikenna and Delmi, each of them giving Ahnna a significant, though differing, stare from Ikenna's horse before they took off.

In class, in the midst of the novelty of wearing Ikenna's principal, Ahnna felt that she was just finding her bearings when the messenger boys came back, bringing the enormity of the morning to her mind again, and the rest of the school day went by in a haze.

Late that afternoon, Ahnna took up her books and shut up the empty schoolhouse, starting out by herself on a contemplative walk home, but she made it no farther than the lake. She heard an approaching horse and looked up, feeling her heart jump at the sight of Ikenna again riding toward her.

"I thought you returned home with your party," Ahnna told him as he pulled up and dismounted to walk over to her with a smile. Ahnna attempted to reciprocate his smile but was too affected to do so.

"No, I will be leaving for the estate after I take you to the farmhouse. I have been there with your mother most of the afternoon. Was it a good day of class?"

"Was it? I hardly know," Ahnna confessed with a shake of her head. Then she cautiously went on. "Ikenna? You mentioned the Chief of State today. Were you serious about his intention to be at your...to come to the marriage ceremony?"

"I was. I received a letter from the State Escritoire after the war. The Chief expressed his disappointment that I had to miss the honor of being a witness at the signing of the surrender agreement. So I had a reply letter go out from my estate saying that I would be duly honored if the Chief would be a guest at the marriage ceremony I was sure to be having next spring. I got a favorable response from the escritoire about it." Ikenna's smile faded when Ahnna still did not return it. "All I would need was a favorable response from you."

Ahnna stared up at Ikenna, her pulse quickening to a degree that prevented her from mustering up the energy for surprise at his disclosure.

A hint of misgiving was trickling into Ikenna's look. "Ahnna? I know this all might be something of a shock to you. But are you displeased by it?"

"What? Oh, dear, no. I am in no way displeased." Ahnna closed her eyes. "Forgive me," she appealed to Ikenna, her eyes reopening as she gave up on her bearings altogether, for the day. "I am thinking of something else. I do not know if I am supposed to articulate this, while I am as yet overwhelmed by you and everything you have said and done. But on the occasion when you first paid suit to me—well, you were so beautiful about it, and even in my awkward rejection of it, a part of me wished that you might have, um, that you might have finished what..."

Ahnna's voice drifted off then, as Ikenna was already taking her books out of her hands, stooping to stack them carefully on the ground before he straightened back up. "Naturally," he said. "I hope it was not selfish of me not to want to share this part with our theatre audience, earlier. I have been imagining it ever since that night you persuaded me to go to sleep by kneeling right at my head, with your hair spilling over your shoulders, much as it is now."

Ahnna felt a flush coming on at the idea that she could have so stimulated a wounded warrior while she'd been serving as his nurse. Yet, she had no time to dwell on any embarrassment as Ikenna readily closed the bit of distance between them. His hands slid around her, drawing her into an embrace accentuated and heated by his impassioned kiss on her mouth, a kiss that soundly, marvelously drove the wind out of her. Her lips agreed with his, and she might not have been able to remain on her feet if she hadn't accordingly embraced Ikenna back, no part of her regretting the "fire, fire indeed" present between them.

When the time would come, Ahnna would miss her mother. She would miss being so physically near all that reminded her of her father, and she would hope for the chance to see Hsiu Mei and her pupils again. She would have much to learn as the mistress of a tradesman's estate, but if she'd been taught anything by her upbringing and the war, she'd been taught how to adapt to a new station.

And, years ahead, when she would take customary springtime walks with Ikenna through the blossoming trees in their gardens; when she would paint pictures of their village; when she would tutor the increasing number of the estate party members' children, as well as her own; when she would accompany Ikenna to conferences and banquets with the Chief of State and national and regional administrators; and when she would revise Ikenna's speeches for emphasis and clarity before he delivered them, or when she would stand and join him in speaking to their fellow countrymen and women looking for guidance in navigating their collective independence, she would, overall, find ways to carry all of it out in graciousness, without apology.

At last she awakens to a new reality...
Don't miss the sequel to
Eminence

Simplicity

To find all of Nadine's books and her blog featuring book reviews as well as posts on writing, diversity, films, and more, visit:

www.prismaticprospects.wordpress.com